7/98

 St. Louis Community College

Forest Park
Florissant Valley
Meramec

Instructional Resources
St. Louis, Missouri

The Tortilla Cat

NANCY WILLARD

ILLUSTRATED BY

JEANETTE WINTER

HARCOURT BRACE & COMPANY
San Diego ❦ New York ❦ London

Requests for permission to make copies of any part of the work should be mailed to:
Permissions Department, Harcourt Brace & Company,
6277 Sea Harbor Drive,
Orlando, Florida 32887-6777.

Library of Congress Cataloging-in-Publication Data
Willard, Nancy.
The tortilla cat/written by Nancy Willard; illustrated by Jeanette Winter. — 1st ed.
p. cm.
Summary: When all five Romero children get sick, a magical cat appears
in the night and cures them of their fevers.
ISBN 0-15-289587-6
[1. Sick—Fiction. 2. Single-parent family—Fiction.
3. Cats—Fiction. 4. Magic—Fiction.] I. Winter, Jeanette, ill. II. Title
PZ7.W6553To 1998
[Fic]—dc20 95-45731

First edition
A C E F D B

Printed in Singapore

The illustrations in this book were done in acrylics
on Strathmore Bristol paper.
The display type was set in Pabst Oldstyle.
The text type was set in Perpetua.
Color separations by United Graphic Pte Ltd
Printed and bound by Tien Wah Press, Singapore
This book was printed on totally chlorine-free
Nymolla Matte Art paper.
Production supervision by Stanley Redfern and Ginger Boyer
Designed by Jeanette Winter and Judythe Sieck

There was once a doctor who could cure anything. That's what people said. Warts? Flu? Chicken pox?

"Go to Doctor Romero. He can cure anything."

The doctor and his wife, Catherine, had five children. Anna was eleven, Maria was ten, Tony was nine, and the twins, Michael and Thomas, were six. The children shared the affections of five goldfish. They would have preferred something furry with four feet, but Doctor Romero announced he did not want fleas in the carpet and hairs on his trousers. Goldfish do not bark or shed or chew shoes or bring home small dead animals. They do not beg to be walked in cold weather.

And such cold weather it was! With the cold
weather came a fever worse than any Doctor Romero
had ever seen. His waiting room was filled with
people, old and young, rich and poor. None of his
medicines worked against this fever. Some people got
well, some got worse, some died.

Among those who died was his wife, Catherine. As
the snow fell on her new grave, the doctor gathered
his children around him and wept.

"Who will take care of us now?" cried Tony.

Doctor Romero shook his head.

"I'll do my best, but I'm counting on you to help,
Anna, because you're the oldest."

The snow fell, the ice glittered on the puddles, the time passed, and Doctor Romero did his best to be both father and mother to his children. Every night he tucked them into bed and kissed them, just the way their mother had done, before he went to bed himself.

One night, long after the doctor had kissed the children good night, Anna woke up. She was sure she heard someone crying outside. She climbed out of bed, tiptoed downstairs, and opened the front door. There on the doorstep sat a little gray cat.

The cat stepped into the warm vestibule and trotted straight up the stairs to the room Anna and Maria shared, just as if she knew the way, and found a comfortable place for herself next to Anna's pillow and purred. Anna shook Maria.

"Wake up! We have a cat."

Maria slept on. Then Anna said to herself, *I can have the cat to myself for this night,* and she crawled back into her own bed and fell asleep and dreamed that her mother was calling her for school till she heard Maria in the hall shouting.

"Tony, it's my turn!" called Maria. "You've been in the bathroom for hours."

Anna ran out and grabbed her arm.

"Where's the cat?"

"What cat?" asked Maria.

"The cat that came into our room last night."

Maria stared at her.

"There was no cat in our room."

"There was too," cried Anna. "It was sleeping right next to my pillow."

The bathroom door opened.

"Cat?" cried Tony. "We have a cat?"

Michael and Thomas ran downstairs shouting, "We have a cat!"

"No, we don't," said Maria.

"We did have a cat," said Anna. She was not so sure anymore.

Doctor Romero drove the children to school. He listened to Anna's story of the cat.

"You dreamed it," he said. And he thought how fortunate for him that the children did not have a cat but five goldfish that did not yowl or scratch or bring home small dead animals or beg to be let in, in cold weather.

And such cold weather it was. The air numbed your face and froze your feet and crackled your breath into crystals. On a Monday morning Anna woke up hot and feverish, so full of aches and pains she could not get out of bed. Her father took one look at her and moved Maria into the guest room. He stood at Anna's bedside and peered down at her with sorrowful eyes.

"You have the fever. I will bring you anything you want to eat or drink."

He brought her ginger ale, he brought her chicken soup, but Anna's fever grew worse and worse, and one night Maria tiptoed into her sister's room and said, "Don't die, Anna. Don't die."

"Who says I'm going to die?" whispered Anna, and opened her eyes.

Maria was gone, and Anna watched the empty doorway, hoping her sister would come back. A light was gathering, and as Anna watched it, she caught a delicious fragrance of oregano and thyme.

Suddenly out of the light and into the room stepped the little gray cat. She was walking on her hind legs and carrying a red tray on which rested a single tortilla. And as she walked, the cat sang:

Chimi Chimi Changa,
Choco Yanga.
Jimica, Wamica,
Mammawanna boo.

The cat touched the tortilla to Anna's lips. Instantly the girl felt so hungry, she reached out and snatched the tortilla from the plate and gobbled it up. The cat watched her closely. When Anna had eaten the tortilla and said "Thank you," the cat tucked the tray under her paw and scampered out of the room.

The next morning when Doctor Romero came to check on his daughter, he was astounded to find her sitting up in bed, reading. He took her temperature and found the fever was entirely gone.

"It's a miracle," said Doctor Romero.

"No, it's a cat," said Anna.

"What cat?"

"The cat I told you about. It brought me the most wonderful dinner."

"Cat?" cried Tony at the door. "We have a cat?"

The other children rushed into the room. Michael and Thomas shouted, "We have a cat!"

"Where is this cat?" demanded Maria.

"It went away," said Anna.

Doctor Romero gathered his children around him and stroked his daughter's hair.

"My dear children, when people are very sick, they imagine their dreams are real. The cat Anna saw in her delirium helped her get well. It doesn't matter that it wasn't a real cat."

"The cat was real," said Anna. "I saw it go out that door. It gave me a tortilla to eat and I got well."

In the door, out the door, and two days later, on a Thursday, Maria woke up hot and feverish.

"Time to rise and shine," said Anna. "We'll be late for school."

"I'm sick," said Maria. "Call Papa."

Papa did not need the thermometer to know what ailed Maria.

"You have the fever," he said. "Can I bring you anything to eat or drink?"

"No," whispered Maria.

He brought her ginger ale, he brought her apple juice, but Maria was far sicker than Anna had been. He sat by her bedside and held the straw to her lips and said, "You must drink something. You must."

But Maria did not have the strength to sip through a straw. And one night Tony tiptoed into his sister's room.

"Don't die, Maria."

"Does Papa say I'm going to die?" whispered Maria.

"He doesn't say it. But he's bought a black dress for Anna and black suits for me and Michael and Thomas."

Maria opened her eyes wide. Tony was gone. Light gathered in the empty doorway, a delicious fragrance of oregano and thyme filled the air, and into the room stepped the little gray cat. She was holding a green tray on which rested a single tortilla, and she was singing:

Chimi Chimi Changa,
Choco Yanga,
Jimica, Wamica,
Mammawanna boo.

The cat balanced the tortilla on her paw and wafted it in front of Maria, who sat up at once. She had never felt so hungry in her life. She grabbed the tortilla and crammed it into her mouth.

"Pank 'ou," said Maria. She tried to apologize for speaking with her mouth full, but the cat bowed, laid a cautionary paw on her lips, and left the room bearing the empty tray.

Early the next morning, Maria jumped out of bed and ran into her papa's bedroom shouting—"I'm well!"

Doctor Romero put on his dressing gown, popped a thermometer into her mouth, waited three minutes, and took it from her and read it.

"The fever is gone!" he exclaimed. "Another miracle."

"No, Papa, it was the cat."

And Maria told him how a cat had come into her room carrying a green tray with a tortilla on it, and how she had eaten it and felt ever so much better.

"It was a red tray," called Anna from the hall.

"Green," said Maria.

"Red," said Anna.

"Green."

"Red."

"My dear girls," said Doctor Romero, "there was no cat in this house last night. The delusion that a cat is serving a tortilla is one of the peculiarities of this sickness. It should be written up in the medical journals."

"What's *delusion?*" asked Thomas, running into the room.

"Anna and Maria think the cat in their dreams is real. That's a delusion."

"I want to be sick so I can see the cat," said Tony.

"Don't say that," said Doctor Romero. "We've had enough sickness in this family."

But Tony said it again, and that night, which was Wednesday, he put himself to bed early. Michael crept into his room and asked, "Are you really sick or just pretending?"

Tony said nothing.

"Are you just pretending so you can see the cat?"

Tony said, "I feel like I'm burning up."

Doctor Romero was in his study working on an article called "The Tortilla Cat Delusion as a Sign of Recovery" when Michael tugged at his sleeve.

"Tony is sick," he said.

"I wonder if any of us will escape this illness," said the doctor. He rose and put aside his article and hurried into Tony's room. Tony had climbed into bed with his clothes on, and Doctor Romero helped him into his pajamas and tucked him in.

"Can I bring you anything?"

Tony shook his head.

"Anna and Maria have promised to look in on you."

"Papa, what if the cat doesn't come?"

Doctor Romero smiled down at his son.

"The cat seems to be a regular visitor in people's dreams here. Perhaps we've inherited a tendency toward the Tortilla Cat Delusion."

"If the cat doesn't come, I'll die, won't I?" whispered Tony.

"What an idea!" exclaimed Doctor Romero, and kissed his son good night.

Yes, what an idea, he told himself on the way back to his own room, and cold shivers ran through him. No cat had visited the dreams of his beloved wife, Catherine.

He went to bed, but sleep would not come, and at last he rose, put on his dressing gown, and tiptoed into Tony's room. To his astonishment he found Michael and Thomas fast asleep on either side of him. He touched Michael's forehead, then Thomas's.

"They have all got the fever," he said.

He pulled Tony's reading chair from his desk to the side of his bed.

"I will keep watch," he whispered. "Nothing can hurt you as long as I am here."

But he knew in his heart that keeping watch over children does not save them. He had sat at the bedside of many a patient he could not save. He stared at the flushed faces of his children. Perhaps even now they were dreaming of the magic cat. And then a new fear entered his head.

What if the cat won't come into their dreams while I am sitting here? he thought. Yet he could not tear himself away. Outside the window, a new moon signed the night with a sickle.

Doctor Romero did not remember falling asleep in the chair, only waking up in it. The sun was splashing the room with light. Tony and Michael and Thomas were tugging at him.

"The cat came! She brought me a tortilla on a yellow tray!" cried Tony.

"Orange," said Michael.

"Blue," said Thomas.

"Yellow," said Tony.

"Green!" called Maria.

"Red!" shouted Anna.

At breakfast the children talked of nothing but the wonderful cat. Doctor Romero was so happy to see his family well again that he never said a word against the cat, until Anna remarked, "I wonder if we'll ever see the cat again?"

"The Tortilla Cat Delusion," said Doctor Romero. "I wonder if any of my other patients have seen the Tortilla Cat?"

"It's not a delusion," said Anna.

"It's real," said Tony. "Why won't you believe us?"

"Because if I believed in a cat that brings tortillas in the night and makes people well, the universe would be much more complicated than it is now," said Doctor Romero. "It's complicated enough learning to be a doctor."

Thursday and Friday the doctor worked so late in the office that the children had to get their own supper. They sent out for pizza, which pleased all of them except Michael, who did not like anchovies.

In the morning Doctor Romero checked on his patients in the hospital. In the afternoon he saw patients in his office. The waiting room was full.

He had promised to take the children out for a Chinese dinner on Saturday and then to a movie. But at four in the afternoon he felt so weak and hot that he closed the office early and went home and crawled into bed. One by one the children tiptoed into his room, and when he opened his eyes, they were standing in a ring around him.

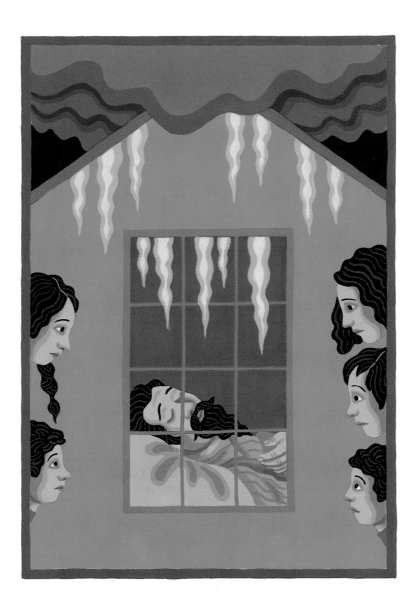

"I believe I've got the fever myself," he said.

"I will bring you anything you want to eat or drink," said Anna.

"Are you really sick or just pretending?" asked Michael.

"Don't die, Papa," said Maria. "Don't die."

At these words Thomas began to wail.

"Who says I'm going to die?" whispered Doctor Romero. "The cat will come with a tortilla on a red tray and I'll be well again."

"Green," said Maria.

"Yellow," said Tony.

"Orange," said Michael.

"Blue," said Thomas.

"But what if the cat doesn't come?" asked Tony.

Maria brought her father a glass of ginger ale and held the straw to his lips. "You have to drink this," she said. "You have to."

Tony lugged his chair, and his notebook and pencil, into the room, and pushed it close to his father's bed and sat down to draw him.

"I appreciate your concern," whispered the doctor. "Can you take care of yourselves until I'm well? I'm counting on you, Anna, because you're the oldest. Tony, will you put your drawing on the nightstand where I can see it?"

"It's a picture of you taking care of the cat," said Tony. "I haven't drawn the cat yet."

The drawing showed Doctor Romero holding his stethoscope and listening to the air. As they tiptoed out of his room, tears sprang to his eyes. *What will happen to these children if I don't get well?* he asked himself. The possibility was too terrible to think of. Yet as he felt himself burning with fever, he could not help thinking of it.

A light wind breathed through the room and blew Tony's drawing to the floor. Doctor Romero tried to pick it up but found he had no strength in his hands at all, and this frightened him very much.

"If there really is a Tortilla Cat, I wish she would come to me now," murmured Doctor Romero, and he thought how wonderful the universe would be if it had room for such a cat.

In the doorway a light was gathering and bringing with it the fragrance of oregano and thyme. And then, to the doctor's great astonishment, a little gray cat stepped out of the light into the room and walked straight to his bedside. She was carrying a golden tray on which rested a single tortilla, and she was singing:

Chimi Chimi Changa,
Choco Yanga,
Jimica, Wamica,
Mammawanna boo.

How deftly she balanced the tray on one paw and with the other brought the tortilla to his lips. After the first bite the doctor found he could lift his hands, and he plucked the tortilla from her paw and gobbled it up and felt the fever leave him.

The cat was gone.

The doctor lay wide awake and amazed. What was that noise? Someone was crying. He climbed out of bed, stepped into the hall, and listened at the door of Anna and Maria's room. Silence. Then he listened at Tony's door. Silence. He peeked into Michael and Thomas's room. The twins were fast asleep under the comforter.

Someone outside was crying. The doctor crept downstairs and opened the front door. There on the welcome mat sat five kittens: one gray, one orange, one tabby, one black-and-white, and one calico.

Doctor Romero took a deep breath before he gathered them into the hem of his dressing gown and carried them upstairs. At the foot of Tony's bed he left the black-and-white one.

Chimi Chimi Changa, said a voice in the doctor's head.

At the foot of the bed Michael and Thomas shared, he left the orange kitten and the gray one.

Choco and Yanga, said the voice.

Through a crack in the door of Maria and Anna's room, the doctor slipped the calico and the tabby.

Jimica and Wamica, said the voice.

"If your mother ever returns to see how her kittens are faring, I shall call her Mammawanna Boo," said the doctor to Jimica and Wamica.

And he went into his study to work on his article.
Hastily he changed the title from "The Tortilla Cat
Delusion" to "The Tortilla Cat." He wrote page after
page as the sun rose and he waited for his children to
wake up.